Big Bird Meets Santa Claus

Featuring Jim Henson's Sesame Street Muppets

By Liza Alexander
Illustrated by Tom Brannon

Originally published in a slightly longer version titled
Imagine . . . Big Bird Meets Santa Claus

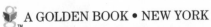

A GOLDEN BOOK • NEW YORK

Published by Golden Books Publishing Company, Inc., in cooperation with Children's Television Workshop

Library of Congress Catalog Card Number: 96-77530   ISBN: 0-307-98814-7   MCMXCVII

A portion of the money you pay for this book goes to Children's Television Workshop.
It is put right back into SESAME STREET and other CTW educational projects. Thanks for helping!

It's Christmastime on Sesame Street! Today we're trimming the tree. My favorite ornament is a tiny Santa Claus with reindeer and a sleigh.

I sure would like to *meet* Santa. Wouldn't you? I wonder what Santa's doing right now.

Santa lives at the North Pole. Maybe at this very moment he's decorating *his* tree, or maybe he's hanging a Christmas wreath on his door.

If I went to the North Pole, I could meet Santa Claus. He would invite me into his house. Santa would ask me to help him get ready for Christmas.

Santa's workshop is downstairs, way below ground. There are rooms for making every different kind of toy in the world.

Santa shows me around. In the office I say, "Hello, Mrs. Claus. Pleased to meet you!" Mrs. Claus is in charge of Santa's mail. The elves use fancy computers to keep track of which child has asked for what present.

Mrs. Claus shows me the letter that I helped Elmo write! He wants a doll for Christmas. Elmo loves dolls.

Santa takes me to the workroom where the elves are making Elmo's present.

Then Santa shows me a doll that looks just like him. "Very handsome," he says. "Ho, ho, ho!"

I laugh. Santa Claus sure is a jolly old fellow.

In the next workroom the elves are building wagons and
bicycles and roller skates.

Santa asks me to be a test driver. I strap on a new pair of
roller skates and I'm off! Wheeeeeee!

It's time to tidy up the wrapping room. I use a wagon to help the elves. This is the most beautiful trash I've ever seen. Oscar would be amazed!

Next I take a shiny new unicycle for a spin. I ride through the elves' bunk room . . .

and into the reindeer stable. The reindeer give me some funny looks. They've probably never seen a bird on a unicycle before!

Now I cycle into the gym. There's Santa! He exercises every day. Santa has to keep trim so that he can slide down chimneys.

When Santa goes to change, he lets me try on his Santa costume. Look at me! I'm Santa Bird. Ho, ho, ho!

Santa takes me to the Clauses' comfy sitting room for a snack.

Mrs. Claus asks me about Sesame Street. "It's wonderful," I tell her. "I have lots of friends, and my own cozy nest, and a dog named Barkley. . . ."

Suddenly I realize that I want to go home! I don't want to miss Christmas on Sesame Street! But how am I going to get there?

It's silly of me to worry. Even though Christmas is coming and Santa is very busy, he offers to take me home to Sesame Street! I thank Santa and Mrs. Claus and say good-bye.

Then around the world Santa and I fly, through the big starry night, reindeer and sleigh and all!

And here I am, back on Sesame Street. "Ho, ho, ho!" I chuckle loudly.

"Big Bird," says Elmo, "you sound just like Santa Claus." I chuckle even louder. Merry Christmas, everyone!